Visitors to London, both from abroad and from elsewhere in Britain, put Madame Tussaud's at the head of the list of places they must see. But what of the woman whose energy, brain and skilful hands created this world famed institution? The story of her life and work is fascinating.

Acknowledgments
The author and publishers wish to acknowledge the considerable help of Miss Juliet Simpkins and Miss Undine Concannon of Madame Tussaud's in the preparation of this book.
Illustrative material is acknowledged as follows: Aviation Photographs International, page 34 (bottom); Peter Dennis, illustrations on cover, and pages 12/13, 21, 22; Mary Evans Picture Library, page 29 (top left); Robert Harding Picture Library, pages 8/9 (top); The Historical Museum, Berne, pages 4/5; The Hulton-Deutsch Collection, pages 11, 34; The Mansell Collection, page 12; National Portrait Gallery, pages 20, 29 (top), 30 (centre); Mick Usher, illustration on page 18; all other photographs and prints by courtesy of Madame Tussaud's.
Book designed by R W Ditchfield.

British Library Cataloguing in Publication Data
Daly, Audrey
   The story of Madame Tussaud.
   1. Wax model human figures. Making.
Tussaud, Marie
   I. Title   II. Series
   736'.93
   ISBN 0-7214-1091-X

First edition

Published by Ladybird Books Ltd Loughborough Leicestershire UK
Ladybird Books Inc Auburn Maine 04210 USA
© LADYBIRD BOOKS LTD MCMXC
Printed in England

The story of
Madame Tussaud

by AUDREY DALY

Ladybird Books

*I*n December 1761, the child who was to become the world famous Madame Tussaud was christened Anna Maria Grosholtz. She was the daughter of Joseph Grosholtz, a soldier who died before she was born.

*M*arie, as she was known, was little more than a baby when her mother became housekeeper to Dr Philippe Curtius in the Swiss town of Berne.

*D*r Curtius was already running a small waxwork museum as well as treating patients. Shortly after Marie and her mother arrived, he was asked to go to Paris by the Prince de Conti. Royalty in those days often acted as patrons or sponsors to artists and other creative people. Dr Curtius went, leaving his housekeeper and her daughter behind.

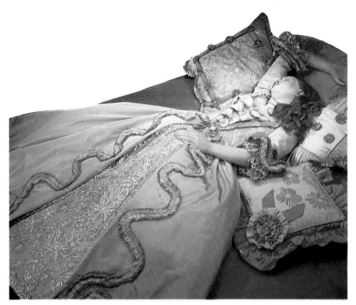

Madame du Barry, favourite of King Louis XV of France, was modelled by Dr Curtius when she was twenty two years old and her portrait still survives as the Sleeping Beauty. Madame du Barry was beheaded in 1793 during the French Revolution. One reason for this was that she wore mourning when the king died. Curtius also made a death mask of her

*The Swiss town of Berne
when Marie Tussaud lived there*

Once settled in Paris, Dr Curtius quickly became successful, modelling, among others, the French king and queen. He also produced pictures in enamel that were much sought after.

By the time that the doctor sent for his housekeeper and her daughter to come to Paris in 1767, Marie was six years old. Fortunately she was a healthy child. Paris in those days was a dirty, smelly place. Infection thrived, and weaker people died.

Marie grew up with an observant eye, and such a gift for model making that Philippe Curtius began to teach her his craft. He trained her in anatomy as well as in taking plaster casts and tinting wax.

At seventeen, Marie was so talented that she modelled the great French writer and philosopher Voltaire

She was lucky enough to meet many famous people at Curtius's *Salon de Cire*, as the wax exhibition was called. There were statesmen, philosophers, and royalty from many countries. Gustavus III of Sweden came to be modelled, and so did the son of Catherine the Great of Russia, as well as Spanish and Prussian princes.

The American statesman Benjamin Franklin was the first to suggest the use of lightning conductors to protect buildings. This likeness made by Madame Tussaud can still be seen today

This wax miniature of Voltaire by Dr Curtius remains on display

Living at Versailles

*W*hen Marie was twenty, her life changed
dramatically. The princess known as Madame
Elizabeth, younger sister of Louis XVI, had
visited the wax exhibition and been very
impressed by Marie's skill as a modelmaker. As
a result, Marie went to live at the Palais de
Versailles as art tutor to the princess. She spent
nine happy years in the rich magnificent world
of the French royal family.

*W*hile Marie was at Versailles, she modelled a
group of the royal family, and these figures are
still to be seen in Madame Tussaud's,
as shown below.

*T*hen life in France began to change. People were hungry and thousands were out of work. They became angry about the way rich people lived. As the first mutterings of the French Revolution began, Dr Curtius decided that Marie would be safer in Paris.

The French royal family at dinner. Members of the public could go and watch if they wanted to

*M*adame Elizabeth was sad to see her go. She gave her the furniture from Marie's own room at Versailles as a parting present.

These two chairs came from Marie's room at Versailles

Versailles, home of the French royal family

Back in Paris, Marie was in a different world yet again.

Dr Curtius was a revolutionary, and the talk at his dinner table was all of changing the government of France.

The people that Marie began to meet were quite different from the wealthy gentlefolk she had known so far. They had few manners, but very strong opinions about politics. Even some of those who were well born, such as the Duc d'Orleans (uncle of King Louis XVI), were against the aristocracy that ruled France. Danton, one of the first leaders of the French Revolution, was amongst Curtius's new friends.

Dr Curtius

This cartoon was called Change the Heads!
It appeared in 1787, showing that the French people
were already calling for a new type of government

*T*hen came a very important day in French people's lives – 14th July 1789. This day is still the French national holiday, celebrating the fall of the Bastille and the start of the French Revolution.

*O*ne of the earliest victims of the Revolution was the governor of the Bastille. After his head had been paraded through Paris on a pike, a wax death mask was made and put on show.

Although the Bastille is often used as a symbol of the way French people were kept down by the aristocracy, really it was just a prison – with very few prisoners in it. Dr Curtius, leading a troop of the National Guard, helped to storm the Bastille on that famous day

Terror stalks the streets

*T*he next few years were troubled ones for the people of Paris. France's new leaders changed many things. They gave the government control over the Church, and took away the king's power. Then, when the king and his queen Marie Antoinette tried to leave the country, they were brought back. Later they were put to death.

Marie Antoinette on her way to the guillotine – a sketch made by an eye-witness

A Tribunal was set up to punish people who were against the revolutionary government. People from every walk of life went to the guillotine.

*A*lthough Dr Curtius was friendly with most of the new leaders, Marie must have known that their safety might not last. On at least one occasion Dr Curtius used his influence to help a friend in need. He bribed the 'incorruptible' Robespierre to release his showman friend Philipstal from prison.

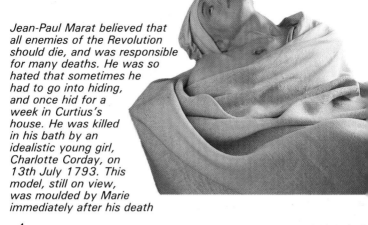

Jean-Paul Marat believed that all enemies of the Revolution should die, and was responsible for many deaths. He was so hated that sometimes he had to go into hiding, and once hid for a week in Curtius's house. He was killed in his bath by an idealistic young girl, Charlotte Corday, on 13th July 1793. This model, still on view, was moulded by Marie immediately after his death

At last the government turned on its own members. Danton, who had often dined with Curtius, was condemned to death.

The death masks of Louis XVI and Marie Antoinette, and an actual guillotine blade

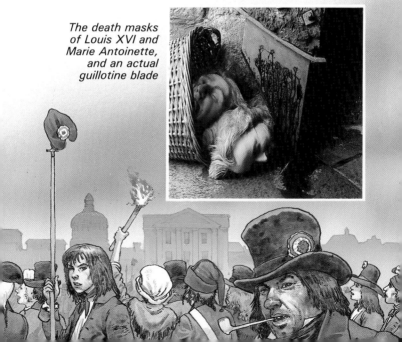

A prisoner for a week

Danger struck suddenly, at a time when Dr Curtius was away. Marie, her mother and her aunt were all arrested and taken to prison. No one knew why – people could be arrested just for sympathising with a victim of the guillotine.

Marie found herself sharing a room with nineteen other women. They had nothing to sleep on but dirty straw, the food was uneatable, and they were all forced to have their hair cut to be ready for the guillotine.

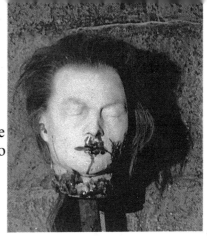

Marie's death mask of Robespierre

*W*hile in prison, Marie met Josephine de Beauharnais, who later became the Empress Josephine, wife of Napoleon Bonaparte.

*T*he three women of Curtius's household were set free in about a week. Again, they didn't know why. Too frightened to go back to their home, they went to stay with a friend until Dr Curtius returned to Paris.

*B*ut the end of the Years of Terror was near. Robespierre, the most powerful of Curtius's friends, who had condemned so many, was himself executed. The long tyranny was over.

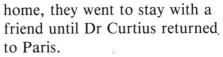

Some of the death masks that were made during this terrible time still exist. They include that of the Public Prosecutor, Fouquier-Tinville, the last guillotined head that Marie moulded

*W*ith the end of the Revolution came other changes. First, in 1794, Dr Curtius died, leaving Marie three houses and the prosperous *Cabinet de Cire*. She put his affairs in order, then moved on to run the exhibition efficiently.

*M*arie Grosholtz was far ahead of her time in many ways. She was very much a business woman. She knew that the exhibition had to make a profit, and had also to be kept up to date. Because public feeling had changed, she had all the figures of revolutionaries removed from the display.

A smaller but equally important detail (Marie always kept her eye on the smallest details) was the way the doormen were dressed. During the Revolution for example they had often been dressed as National Guards. Now she made

A model of the time —
the 34 stone Paul Butterbrodt

them dress like members of a new political party, the 'Gilded Youth'.

*T*he next year, 1795, turned out to be outstanding. Marie married François Tussaud, a civil engineer several years younger than herself. And a young general, Napoleon Bonaparte, began to make a name for himself.

A nineteenth century artist's impression of the Cabinet de Cire *in Paris*

Napoleon

*M*arie Tussaud and her husband soon started a family, but their first child died at six months old. Later Marie had two sons, Joseph and François, usually called Francis.

*E*ven in those early years, married life took second place to Marie Tussaud's career, and she continued to work hard modelling France's new rulers. A great moment came in 1799, when Napoleon

Josephine Bonaparte

became First Consul and his wife Josephine persuaded him to sit for Madame Tussaud. Napoleon was so pleased with the result that he sent two of his generals to be modelled as well.

*A*lthough the exhibition was still popular, there were fewer visitors. At this time, Curtius's friend Philipstal was in Paris on a visit. His Phantasmagoria show had been very successful in London, and he thought that Marie Tussaud's collection might also do well there.

*S*o towards the end of 1802, Madame Tussaud and her four year old son Joseph went to London. The rest of the family stayed behind.

Napoleon's minister of foreign affairs, Talleyrand-Perigord, who later became Grand Chamberlain

Madame Tussaud was now in partnership with Monsieur Philipstal. This was a mistake from the start, since his actions proved he was not the friend she had always thought him. When he advertised his show at the Lyceum Theatre,

King George III

for example, her own exhibition was never mentioned. Nor would he help with her expenses, which were heavy.

*B*ut in spite of the difficulties Philipstal put in her way, Marie's reputation began to grow. An early opportunity came when a traitor, Colonel Despard, was hanged and then beheaded for his part in a plot to murder the English king, George III. Marie modelled him and put him on show – and business improved. Later she was asked to model the Duchess of York, wife of the king's second son. This was her first royal commission in Britain.

*W*hen the booking at the Lyceum came to an end, Philipstal decided to take the show to Scotland. Marie agreed to go on ahead. She packed her precious models and set forth by sea for Edinburgh, taking her small son with her.

*O*nce in business for herself, Marie was even more determined to be successful.

*S*he took her exhibition all over Britain in search of new audiences. She opened in towns like Sheffield, Stafford and York when the trade fairs were on, because there were always plenty of visitors at those times.

*T*ransporting as many as seventy full length richly dressed figures from town to town was no easy matter, even though the roads had

for example, her own exhibition was never mentioned. Nor would he help with her expenses, which were heavy.

*B*ut in spite of the difficulties Philipstal put in her way, Marie's reputation began to grow. An early opportunity came when a traitor, Colonel Despard, was hanged and then beheaded for his part in a plot to murder the English king, George III. Marie modelled him and put him on show – and business improved. Later she was asked to model the Duchess of York, wife of the king's second son. This was her first royal commission in Britain.

*W*hen the booking at the Lyceum came to an end, Philipstal decided to take the show to Scotland. Marie agreed to go on ahead. She packed her precious models and set forth by sea for Edinburgh, taking her small son with her.

Only one person enjoyed the voyage north – young Joseph, who found it all great fun.

It was however a stormy uncomfortable trip, with Marie more fearful for the safety of her models than herself. During the next thirty or so years travelling, either by sea or on badly made roads, her first task on arrival was always to repair any damage done. This was daunting even for Marie, because both heads and clothes often had to be made good again.

*B*y the time she arrived in Edinburgh, Madame Tussaud's contract with Philipstal had become a great liability. He would not help with her heavy travelling expenses, and he continued to take half her earnings. A lawyer advised her that the contract could not be broken.

*B*ut her exhibition was proving very popular, first in Edinburgh, then in Dublin. At last – in Dublin – she managed to scrape together the money to buy out her partner.

Edinburgh

*O*nce in business for herself, Marie was even more determined to be successful.

*S*he took her exhibition all over Britain in search of new audiences. She opened in towns like Sheffield, Stafford and York when the trade fairs were on, because there were always plenty of visitors at those times.

*T*ransporting as many as seventy full length richly dressed figures from town to town was no easy matter, even though the roads had

improved. She continued to add new figures of people in the public eye. It took Marie Tussaud only a few hours however to set up her show, often in the spacious Assembly Rooms which most towns had.

During the Bristol Riots of 1831, all the figures had to be moved to a safer place

*O*ne year, when on her way to Dublin, Marie was shipwrecked. But it was not long before she was back at work – this time in Liverpool, where her second son Francis came from Paris to join her.

The Music Hall, Sheffield, where Marie Tussaud exhibited

Marie Tussaud in her touring days

25

Chamber of Horrors

*D*uring the thirty three years in which Marie Tussaud toured Britain, the world famous Chamber of Horrors came into being.

*P*erhaps it really started in Manchester in 1822, where one part of the exhibition was known as the 'peculiarity room'. Later, this became the 'Separate Room', described as 'inadvisable for ladies to visit'. It wasn't until 1846 that the magazine *Punch* christened it the 'Chamber of Horrors'.

*L*ife-serving murderers share the modern day Chamber of Horrors with those of the past, conjuring up a great degree of cruelty and inhumanity, and the punishments that they bring.

The picture opposite shows a Victorian London street at the time of the well known murderer, Jack the Ripper

Remarkable Characters, Subjects, &c.

An old Coquette, who teazed her husband's life out; two beautiful Infants; a small Cabinet of Portraits, in wax, by the celebrated Courcius of Paris, viz.—The dying Philosopher, Socrates; death of Cleopatra, Queen of Egypt; Louis XV. and his Queen; Louis XVI. and Duc d'Orleans; M. Voltaire; Shepherd and Shepherdess.

Biographical and Descriptive Sketches may be had at the Place of Exhibition, price Sixpence.

Madame TUSSAUD, in offering this little Work to the Public, has endeavoured to blend utility and amusement. It contains an outline of the History of each Character represented in the Exhibition, which will not only greatly increase the pleasure to be derived from a mere view of the Figures, but will also convey to the minds of young persons much biographical knowledge, a branch of education universally allowed to be one of the highest importance.

Open every Day from Eleven till Four, and from Half-past Six till Ten

LADIES AND GENTLEMEN ARE REQUESTED NOT TO TOUCH THE FIGURES.

Admittance 1s.—Children under eight years of age, 6d.

Subscribers' Tickets (not transferable) 5s. will admit to the Promenade, &c. during the time the Exhibition remains in Birmingham.

The following highly interesting Figures and Objects, in consequence of the peculiarity of their appearance, are placed in an adjoining situation, and are well worth the attention of Artists and Amateurs; taken by order of the National Assembly, by Madame Tussaud—

The celebrated John Paul Marat, one of the leaders of the French Revolution, taken immediately after his assassination by Charlotte Corde. The following Heads :—Robespierre, Carrier Foquier de Tainville, and Herbert, were taken immediately after execution. The celebrated Count de Lorge, who was confined twenty years in the Bastile, taken from life. Mirabeau.

Also, phrenological Portraits of the Faces of

STEWART AND HIS WIFE,

Who were executed in Edinburgh on the 13th of August, 1829, having confessed to the murder of seven persons by means of POISON, which they familiarly called Doctoring.

Curious and interesting Relics, &c.

The Shirt of Henry IV. of France in which he was Assassinated by Ravaillac, with various Original Documents relative to that transaction. A small Model of the original French Guillotine, with its Apparatus; a model of the Bastile in Paris, in its entire state.

An Egyptian Mummy;

Proved by the Hieroglyphics upon the Swathe, to be the body of the Princess of Memphis, who lived in the Reign of Sesostris King of Egypt, A.M. 2513, 1491 years before Christ, being actually 3321 years old.—Admittance 6d.

‡. ALL KINDS OF OLD-FASHIONED DRESSES, AND PASTE ORNAMENTS BOUGHT.

*E*ventually Marie Tussaud's travels came to an end. She returned to London, setting up her exhibition first in the Old London Bazaar in Gray's Inn Road. It moved three more times before coming to rest in 1835 in The Bazaar, at the corner of Baker Street and Portman Square. There it was to stay for almost fifty years.

*A*mong the new models at this time was the Duke of Wellington, hero of the Battle of Waterloo. He was shown looking at his old enemy, Napoleon Bonaparte. The Duke himself would sometimes come in to smile at the sight of the two of them together.

Napoleon
Bonaparte

Duke of
Wellington

A real tribute to Marie Tussaud's success came from the famous showman Barnum when he tried to buy her exhibition to take to New York

An early portrait of Queen Victoria

*I*n 1836 Marie modelled the Princess Victoria (soon to be Queen) and her mother.

*T*he exhibition was now in a very smart neighbourhood, surrounded by well to do people of the kind that Madame Tussaud always tried to attract. She never forgot she also had a humbler public however, and she held special sessions for the 'labouring classes'.

Always in search of the new and interesting, Marie bought George IV's coronation robes to exhibit. Some still exist

Marie's eldest son Joseph enjoyed making silhouettes, such as this one of the Tussaud family

Prince Albert

*M*arie's sons Francis and Joseph were now middle-aged men with families of their own. They were both skilled modelmakers and a great help in the business. But Marie Tussaud was still very much in charge of her own show, in spite of her advancing years.

*S*oon after Queen Victoria was crowned in 1837, the Exhibition had a superb coronation scene to offer. And when Victoria married

Albert in 1840, Madame Tussaud produced a charming group showing the prince placing the ring on his bride's finger. Then, as now, people were always interested in the royal family.

*B*y this time, Marie had become a celebrity in her own right. She wrote her *Memoirs*. The fame of her waxwork show was complete when it appeared in cartoons and even in one of Charles Dickens' books, *The Old Curiosity Shop*.

*W*hen her husband François died in 1848, Marie Tussaud had not seen him for over forty years. She had neither needed nor missed him, it seemed. She herself died just two years later, in her ninetieth year.

At 81, Madame Tussaud made a portrait of herself which can still be seen

The year of the Great Exhibition dawned – 1851. People came from all over the world to see it, and the Tussaud family went to work as Marie had taught them.

They opened the Hall of Kings, combining wax models with marble sculpture and paintings, in a room said to be the largest in Europe. The Hall paid for its enormous cost within a year.

However, sometimes the family was caught napping. When Charles Dickens died in 1870, there was no model of him. One of Marie's grandsons worked all night to get a portrait ready.

The Exhibition went from strength to strength. In 1890, electricity came along. In 1914, the year the First World War started, the galleries were re-arranged. A huge

Entrance hall

war map was created with lectures to go with it on how the war was going. And there was a cinema!

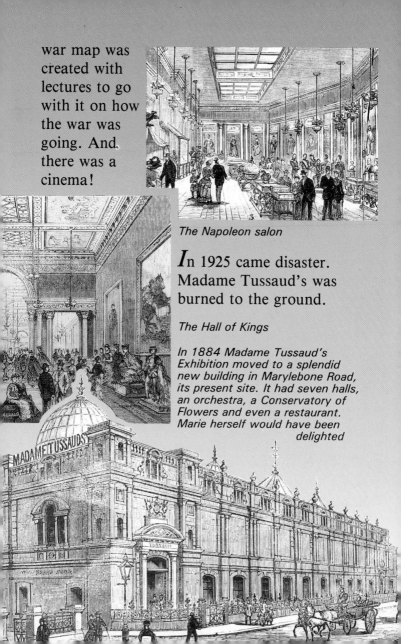

The Napoleon salon

*I*n 1925 came disaster. Madame Tussaud's was burned to the ground.

The Hall of Kings

In 1884 Madame Tussaud's Exhibition moved to a splendid new building in Marylebone Road, its present site. It had seven halls, an orchestra, a Conservatory of Flowers and even a restaurant. Marie herself would have been delighted

It was 1928 before a much enlarged Exhibition opened its doors once more on an eventful era. The dictator Adolf Hitler made his mark in the thirties – and his model was distinctly unpopular.

This model of Princess Elizabeth (now Queen Elizabeth II) was a favourite

When King Edward VIII gave up his throne to marry the American divorcee Mrs Simpson, his speech to the nation was broadcast in the Exhibition.

Edward and Mrs Simpson – the Duke and Duchess of Windsor in 1939

The world grew smaller as air travel became popular, the cinemas were full, and Londoners saw television for the first time.

Then came the Second World War. In 1940 Madame Tussaud's was bombed and some figures were lost.

One of the Spitfires that helped to win the Second World War for Britain

*W*ith peace came some difficulties, but the second half of the century brought new exciting ideas and even greater success. Today over two million people a year flock to an entertainment created by one small determined lady more than two hundred years ago.

When Tussaud's was bombed in 1940, Queen Elizabeth and George VI came to see the bomb crater

Royalty through the ages

*M*adame Tussaud knew her public and gave them just what they wanted. In her day, as now, people were always interested

The royal family in 1990

in those of royal blood, both past and present.

*F*rom William the Conqueror, dour in his plain clothes, through Henry VIII and his six wives, right up to the magnificence of recent royal weddings, Madame Tussaud's today presents a pageant second to none.

Henry VIII
and his wives

When Queen Elizabeth II
was crowned in 1953,
her coronation was
the seventh to be
featured in the history
of the Exhibition

The Hall of Kings in 1968

Entertainment – and education

*T*he waxwork exhibition grew, both in extent and fame, to become the national institution it is today. Nevertheless it has always held closely to Marie Tussaud's original aims: to instruct and to entertain at one and the same time – as splendidly as possible.

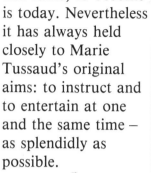

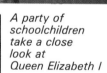

A party of schoolchildren take a close look at Queen Elizabeth I

Charles Dickens, William Shakespeare and Hans Andersen

*A*rtists such as Pablo Picasso and writers from many ages are on show. Shakespeare, gentle Hans Andersen, inimitable Charles Dickens and that queen of crime writers Agatha

Christie can all be seen, as well as another twentieth century writer, Barbara Cartland.

*M*usicians are there as well. Beethoven, seated at the piano, has a half written score in front of him. Mozart is nearby, violin tucked under chin, apparently ready to play a duet.

*M*agician Paul Daniels is another well known figure who doesn't miss a trick.

Famous faces from the entertainment world – Joan Collins, Jimmy Saville, Bob Geldof, Lenny Henry and Paul Hogan

Looking after the details

*I*n line with Marie Tussaud's own quest for perfection, the Exhibition today is kept in order by a whole army of people. Displays are regrouped, and clothes cleaned and mended, or replaced where necessary.

*G*reat care is used in choosing materials. Neither Queen Elizabeth nor Queen Victoria, for example, could have worn clothes made of nylon or acrylic fabrics!

Tidying up the comic actor Eddie Murphy

Recolouring Henry VIII

*H*owever, many models are dressed in clothes that have been worn by the person portrayed. Sometimes, where people remain in the public eye for a number of years, models have to be kept up to date. The model of the first British woman Prime Minister, Margaret Thatcher, has been remodelled four times.

Modelling the tennis player Boris Becker in clay – the first stage following the sitting

*O*ne of the more difficult problems nowadays is choosing who should be modelled. It is considered an honour to be on show, and many people would like to be asked. Just being in the public eye isn't enough, however. Judgment has to be exercised as to how long a particular person will continue to be well known, since his or her likeness will ideally be on view for a long time.

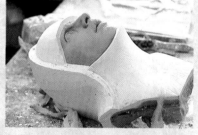

The clay head is moulded in plaster

The head is cast in wax from the plaster mould

The clay body is moulded separately in plaster. The body is cast in fibreglass

*M*ost people give a sitting for their model to be made. But the famous artist Picasso thought that such a good likeness had been made of the artist Rembrandt without a sitting that they didn't need him in person either!

Hair is inserted into the wax scalp. Colour and eyes are also added

The sculptor puts the finishing touches to his model of Boris Becker